The Preacher's Daughter

EMMA BRAY

Chapter One

Heaven

I've long grown accustomed to the silence of my father's church, but today the emptiness seems deafening. The music of the pipe organ, usually so soothing and comforting, echoes off the walls, seeming to mock me with its dissonance. I try to focus my attention on the stained glass windows, depicting the life of Christ, but these too bring despair, as I remember the many sermons my father has given on the subject of obedience, especially to one's parents.

The door to the church opens and I turn. A man steps through. He's wearing a worn leather jacket and a pair of faded jeans. His dark hair is cut close to his head, and his face is ruggedly handsome. He stands just out of the light from the windows, shrouded in shadow, and my heart skips a beat.

The man steps further into the church, and I can see the tattoos that snake up his arms. My eyes widen in surprise.

He's the one all the authorities are looking for—not one of my father's flock—and he's here, in my father's church.

Oh, it's not the tattoos that let me know he's dangerous. I'm not that judgmental, though I know my father and his church are.

No, I've seen this man's face all over the evening news.

He's wanted for murder.

I take an involuntary step back as he walks toward me.

"I don't mean to intrude," he says, his voice low and gruff. "I just...need a place to pray."

I hesitate, unsure of what to make of this man. I've never seen someone who emanates such raw, masculine power in church before, and my father's warnings fill my mind. Yet something in his eyes makes me pause. His eyes hold a mixture of despair and longing, and it draws me to him.

"Go ahead," I finally say, giving him my permission.

The man bows his head and closes his eyes. I watch, transfixed, as he moves his lips silently in prayer. It's crazy, but I feel a strange connection to him and his plea for redemption. He looks so humble...I can't imagine him being guilty of what he's accused of.

When he finishes, he opens his eyes and looks up at me. He doesn't exactly seem peaceful, but his brow isn't furrowed as deeply anymore. His lips part, and he sighs a heavy sigh.

He turns to me, and I see his mouth moving, but I can't hear anything over the sound of my own heart beating in my ears like the thundering hooves of a thousand horses.

The man is rakishly handsome, and his presence is doing funny things to my mind and body.

When I finally come back out of my head, I catch the tail end of his words.

"Thank you," he says softly.

I feel my cheeks flush and clear my throat. "You're welcome."

The man smiles, and it's like the clouds have opened, spilling down upon the land, a rill of rain, so unexpected and intensely beautiful that it's as if each drop was charged with electricity.

My heart flutters. He's so close I can feel the warmth radiating from his body.

I step back, and he steps forward, closing the gap between us.

"My name is Caleb," he rumbles.

Dear God above, his voice is smooth, like melted dark chocolate, with a hint of a rasp, like pouring cream over the top. His words hold a subtle musicality that makes my stomach flutter.

When I speak my own name in response, my voice is quivery but clear. "Heaven Leigh."

"Heaven Leigh," his deep voice rumbles my name as he reaches out and touches my cheek gently. "Heaven," he repeats as he strokes my skin, his voice settling on the shortened version of my name. His fingers are calloused and warm, and I feel myself trembling at his touch.

I decide that I like the way he just calls me 'Heaven' instead of my first name and middle name like everyone else does.

"I'm sorry," he says, withdrawing his hand quickly as if he's been burned. "I shouldn't have done that."

I shake my head. "No, it's okay," I say, my voice barely above a whisper.

Caleb looks into my eyes. I see a longing in them that makes something inside me constrict.

I flush as I feel a sudden heat rise within me. I've never felt this attracted to a man before, like my whole body has become charged. The feeling is strangely familiar, like a memory from another life, long ago, and I feel myself rushing toward its completion.

But that doesn't make any sense because I'm an eighteen-year-old virgin. I've never even kissed a man, much less had sex with one.

Caleb steps closer to me, pressing my back against the wall. His warm breath on my neck sends chills down my spine, and I try to squirm away, but he holds my arms above my head. I'm torn between wanting him to stay and wanting him to go, and the battle in my mind keeps me frozen in place.

"Don't fear me, little one," he breathes, his breath ghosting across my throat and making me tremble with a confusing mixture of excitement and desire.

Caleb's fingers tremble as he fumbles with the buttons on my blouse, and I feel my stomach tightening as he removes my jeans. With a sharp intake of breath, he pulls my panties off and throws them on the floor. I feel exposed and vulnerable as he bares me before him, but at the same time, I can feel a thrill in the air. I *want* him to take me, but I'm also afraid of what might happen.

"Forgive me, Lord, for what I'm about to do," Caleb repents before he leans in and begins to whisper sweet words into my ear as he gently caresses my skin. His touch is gentle but firm, sending waves of pleasure radiating through my body. My heart races, and I feel myself melting into him, his voice a constant companion to the feelings coursing through me.

He kisses me softly, then more passionately as we explore each other with our hands. I gasp at everything he does, responding eagerly to Caleb's every touch. The sensations are overwhelming, pushing me further and further away from reality until it's only the two of us standing alone in front of the altar, alone in our blissful—probably sinful—embrace.

Until suddenly I hear the bang of the church doors opening.

Chapter Two

Caleb

Heaven freezes in my arms, and I internally curse. *Motherfuck!*

My cock is hard as granite, and Heaven is standing here damn near naked as the day she was born.

I shield her with my body and hold a finger up to my lips before I start leading her behind the pulpit where we can hide while she slips her clothes back on.

So much for repentance. I came in here seeking solace yet got lost in this little lamb's luscious body.

I can't help but admire her curves as we try to make our escape.

We quickly make it to the back of the church and I help Heaven dress, then take her hand and lead her out an exit I had noticed earlier. We rush through the streets, trying to avoid being seen by anyone who may recognize us, and I can feel Heaven's trembling fingers in mine. She's scared, but she follows me trustingly, and that fills me with guilt.

She wouldn't be in this situation were it not for me.

What right do I have to put my hands on this innocent little angel? I'm accused of murder. The entire town hates me. I turned to the only place left for me to go, and no sooner do I end up asking the Almighty for forgiveness do I commit another sin.

Damn me for dragging her into this, I think as I lead Heaven through the woods and to my cabin.

I can feel the fear radiating from her as we walk, and so I do my best to reassure her. "It's alright," I say, my voice low and gentle. "You're safe here with me. They've got it all wrong. I'm not guilty of murder."

My words seem to calm her somewhat, and she looks up at me with wide eyes full of questions.

But that's a conversation for another time.

By the time we reach my cabin, Heaven's more relaxed than when we began our journey, but still wary of me. We enter the small wood frame house, and she looks around curiously at everything inside —the furniture made out of tree stumps, the quilts draped across the bed frames hand-stitched by my grandmother years ago, the bookshelves lined with old novels that have been passed down for generations in my family.

The sun is setting outside now, and a warm orange glow fills the room.

"Why have you brought me here?"

"I don't know," I tell her honestly as I spear my fingers through my hair. "I panicked."

"Me too," Heaven agrees softly as she skims her fingertips absently over my countertop. My cock hardens as I imagine that feather-light touch skimming across my aching balls.

"My father would have killed us both if he'd found us like that." She blushes now as she peeks a look at me. "With my clothes off."

"Your father?" I question before the truth hits me like a freight train. "Jesus, you're the preacher's daughter?"

She bites her lips and nods, and I want to facepalm myself. It's bad enough I basically assault an innocent girl I just met, but then I find out she's the preacher's daughter?

Maybe I am the monster they all accuse me of being.

"Did you really kill that man?" her eyes are wide as saucers, her voice barely more than a whisper as she asks the question everyone's dying to know the answer to.

I sigh heavily and try to find the words. "No," I tell her. "I didn't kill him."

Her pretty little brow furrows. "Then why don't you just tell them that?"

"I did."

"And they don't believe you?"

Christ, this girl is so innocent.

"It's not that simple, sweetheart."

The fact of the matter is I know who killed that piece of shit Martin Finley.

It was my sister.

My hands ball into fists when I recall why she hit the fucker on the back of the head with a frying pan so hard she fractured his skull.

The simple fact of the matter is if she hadn't killed him, I would have anyway when I got my hands on him, so I might as well have killed him.

No one hurts my sister.

And there's no way I'm going to throw her under the bus that way. My stomach churns at the thought of exposing her like that and taking away any chance she has of a good life. Even if it means sacrificing my own freedom in the process, family is more important than anything else—and I won't betray my sister by turning her in.

Heaven stares at me for a few moments, then nods slowly as if she understands why I must keep silent.

"Do you believe me?" I ask. For some reason, it's important to me to know if Heaven believes me.

"Yes." Heaven tells me she believes me, blinking up at me with those guileless, innocent, brown eyes, and my throat constricts with sudden emotion.

"I went to the church looking for a miracle, and I found an angel," I marvel as I close the distance between us, drawn to her like a magnet.

Her breath catches and I feel her pulse quicken as I lean in and kiss her softly on the lips, feeling a spark of electricity. Our lips move together in perfect harmony as if we were meant to be together all along.

Fuck, what's wrong with me? Why can't I keep my hands off this girl? From the moment I first saw her, it's been like there's this unyielding force drawing me to her.

She wraps her arms around my neck, pressing

her body against mine, and I can feel the heat radiating from her skin.

Jesus Christ Almighty. I can't believe this sweet little thing is pressing into me like this, kissing me back, *wanting* me too.

We deepen the kiss, each stroke more heated and passionate than the last. A wave of desire washes over me so strong it almost knocks me off my feet.

I pull away slightly and look into Heaven's eyes, which are glazed with lust and heavy with emotion. Her cheeks are flushed a deep rose color that matches perfectly with her luscious red lips.

My heart is hammering in my chest as I realize that this beautiful girl has just given me something no one else ever has—her trust—and it feels like a gift from Heaven itself.

I want to fall to my knees and worship at her feet. Fuck, this girl will be my new religion.

I cup her face in my hands and kiss her again, my tongue mating with hers.

The unpracticed way she whimpers into my mouth and tentatively kisses me back sends precum frothing up out of my tip.

I trail kisses down the delicate column of her neck, feeling her body tremble in anticipation. Her skin is soft and smooth beneath my lips, like velvet. I can feel her heart pounding against my own chest as I make my way down to her collarbone.

I smile against her skin as she gasps and presses herself closer to me.

My hands roam up and down her body, exploring every inch of her curves. Her breathing is becoming more rapid and shallow with each passing moment, sending a rush of heat between my legs that's almost unbearable.

I reach for the hem of her shirt and slide it up over her head, revealing a pair of perky breasts topped with dark nipples that beg for attention. I take one into my mouth and swirl my tongue around it while Heaven moans in pleasure above me.

I move on to the other breast, teasing the tight bud with gentle licks before biting it lightly. Heaven cries out in pleasure and arches into me, pushing herself further into my embrace as I continue to lavish attention on every inch of exposed skin with my lips and tongue.

"Caleb," she breathes my name in a quivering voice that sends my blood surging through my veins. "I've never," her voice falters as I continue to lick and suck on the hardened little peaks of her nipples. "I've never done this before."

Hot damn. I suspected she was a virgin, but hearing the confirmation from her lips is almost enough to make me nut in my pants right here and now.

"I know, sweet girl," I somehow manage to croak out. "You've been saving yourself for your daddy, haven't you?"

Her shocked gasp only makes me groan. I don't know where the hell that came from. I've never had the urge to call myself that before, but the truth of it settles over me.

I was born to be this girl's daddy—the one who's going to protect her and take care of her and satisfy her every need.

"Wh-what did you say?" her eyes are glazed, her cheeks pink, her breath coming shallower and shallower.

"That's right. You heard me, baby. Who's your daddy?"

She lets out a little squeak as I move my hand underneath the band of her pants. My fingers feel her through her panties, and my cock jerks at what I find.

She's soaking fucking wet.

And suddenly nothing else matters. I forget all about what I'm accused of and how my life is a virtual shitshow at the moment.

All that matters now is satisfying the little angel in my arms and showing her just what her daddy can do for her.

And that's just what I'm going to do.

Chapter Three

Heaven

I gasp as he slides two fingers inside me, slowly pumping them in and out while his thumb rubs my clit. I'm already so close to the edge of pleasure that it's almost too much. My body starts to tremble, and I throw my head back in pleasure as an orgasm begins to build within me.

Caleb moves his other hand down to my hips, holding me still as he continues to work his fingers inside of me. His mouth finds mine again, devouring it with a hunger that makes my entire body quiver with anticipation.

"Look at you," he breathes against my lips. "You

perfect fucking angel. You gonna cream all over your daddy's fingers?"

"Oh my god..." I breathe out, my head falling back at both the sensations of his fingers rubbing my clit and stroking up into me and the way his forbidden words send a thrill racing through me.

"Yes, that's it," he talks me through it, encouraging me every step of the way.

The sensations keep building until I can't take it anymore, and then suddenly I'm coming apart in Caleb's arms. He holds onto me tightly while I ride out the wave of pleasure before burying his face in my neck, whispering sweet nothings into my ear as I catch my breath.

It's a few moments later when Caleb finally pulls away from me and meets my gaze with a look of raw male hunger on his face.

"You are so motherfucking perfect," he growls before he kisses me deeply again, his tongue mating with mine.

I'm still trying to process what just happened. It was unlike anything I've ever experienced before—intensely pleasurable yet strangely emotional at the same time.

But my brain short circuits when Caleb lifts me in his arms, his lips still locked onto mine, and wraps my legs around his hips, settling my still-sensitive clit against him.

My eyes widen as I feel how hard and big he is through his pants. My eyes roll back in my head when he starts humping his hips against me, sending fresh waves of pleasure snapping through me.

"Fuck, little girl. You gonna let me stick my big dick in that tight little thing?"

I whimper—in concern or lust I'm not entirely sure.

"Sshh, it's okay," he soothes me in between kisses. "I promise if you just let me in there, I'll make you feel so good, sweetheart. Daddy's going to take care of everything. You'll see."

A wave of trust washes over me as I look up into his chocolate brown eyes. I believe him, and suddenly nothing has ever felt more right than this. It's like my whole life has been leading up to this moment.

"Yes, Daddy," I agree, something beautiful clicking inside me as I call him 'Daddy' for the first time.

Caleb makes a choked sound, his dry humping increasing until his hips are pummeling up against me at a furious pace.

"Gotta stop," he grunts in between humps. "Need to get inside that pretty little thing, but fuck, I gotta lick it first, don't I? Need to taste that little cherry before I pop it."

The next thing I know he's laid me across the bed, and he's on his knees in front of me, his face buried between my legs. He breathes in deeply, his chest expanding as he smells me.

My cheeks flame at the primal move, but it's clear Caleb isn't embarrassed at all. "Smells like mine," he growls before he dives in, his tongue snaking out to lick my folds.

He groans, the sound reverberating against my clit as his tongue flicks over it. I squirm on the bed at the new sensation, but Caleb's strong hands keep me in place as he continues to lap up my juices.

"You taste fucking incredible, baby girl," he groans in between licks. "So sweet, like milk and honey."

I moan and try to turn away from him when I feel his tongue drag up through my slit, but he holds me firm, pinning me down as he laps at my pussy.

I look down at him in shock as he spreads my thighs wider, pushing my knees back and revealing my most intimate parts to his hungry gaze. His hands are gripping my hips, holding me in place as though afraid I might run away.

When I look back down at him, I see his eyes are closed as he laps at my pussy, his tongue dragging through my folds. Slowly his tongue flicks back and forth over my clit, making me squirm in pleasure.

"Give me more of that virgin cream," he moans against my sex, his voice vibrating through my core. "Daddy needs it, baby."

I cry out as his mouth closes around my clit, sucking it into his mouth as his tongue lashes out against it.

"Come on my face," he orders.

My body obeys his order, and I scream, my fingers clutching his head as my entire body quakes with the intensity of my orgasm.

Caleb grunts and growls as he laps up my release. "Good girl," he moans before he finally gives my mound one last kiss before he stands.

His cock is jutting out from his pants, and my eyes widen at the length and girth of it.

"I'm going to eat that pussy for every meal," he growls before he fists his cock and pumps it a few times. "I'll just live off it. All the sustenance your daddy needs."

My legs are still shaking when he steps between them.

"Oh," I moan as he spreads my thighs and lines his cock up with my entrance.

I cry out as I feel the head of his cock press against my virgin entrance.

"Daddy, it feels so big," I whimper, legitimately worried that he's not going to fit.

He smiles at me. "It will fit, baby girl," he promises. "Just relax while daddy takes care of you."

He pushes in a couple more inches before I feel him hit resistance.

My entire body tenses up at the pressure, and I grip his arms tightly, my breathing turning ragged. My god, it feels like he's going to tear me apart!

"Be a good girl and let Daddy fuck, baby," he grunts as he continues pushing himself steadily inside me, the pressure building higher and higher, before he finally rams it all the way inside.

"Oh my God!" I scream as he fills me up. Caleb's cock is huge, and I can feel it stretching me wide.

"Jesus!" Caleb cries out hoarsely, every muscle in his neck taut as he throws his head back in pleasure.

"Oh fuck, oh fuck, oh fuck," he chants. I see his arms straining with the effort it's taking him to hold back. "That thing is squeezing me so tight. Can't sit still, baby. Daddy's got to dick you down hard and fast. I'm sorry, honey, but I just can't help it."

I whimper as he gathers me close then and starts to rock in and out of me—hard and fast.

My body melts into his with an animalistic hunger that begs for more. Every thrust sends a wave of pleasure through me, and I cry out each time, begging him to fuck me harder and deeper. I want him to claim me as his own, and when I finally come undone, I scream out, "Fuck me, Daddy!" with everything that I have.

Caleb's nostrils flare. He turns almost feral as he pumps his hips faster, roaring as he fills me up with his thick cock.

I cry out as I feel my pussy start to clench around him, but Caleb doesn't slow down. He just keeps slamming his dick into me, fucking me harder and harder.

"Come for me, baby," he growls. "Come all over Daddy's cock, baby girl."

I scream, the orgasm ripping through me as I shudder and convulse in his arms. Caleb slows down. Then, still buried deep inside me, he takes my mouth in a searing kiss that threatens to melt me into a puddle of desire. I moan against his lips as he gently rocks into me, coaxing every drop of pleasure out of me until it feels like every cell in my body is singing his name.

I feel Caleb's cock start to twitch inside me and I wonder if this is the end. If this is it, then I'm going to spend the rest of my life wondering what it would have been like to fall over the edge with him.

But then, just like that, he pulls away from me and drops to his knees.

"What are you—" I start to say but then I see him looking at me with that same look in his eyes that I saw before ... That look that tells me I'm about to feel his cock one more time.

"Fucking hell, baby girl," he says through gritted teeth, "you're so fucking beautiful."

He leans forward, kissing my stomach as he spreads my legs wide. He kisses my swollen lips, down to my thighs and calves. I whimper as he makes his way back up my body, stopping to suck and lick at my sensitive pussy lips, before closing his mouth around my clit, sucking hard.

"Caleb!" I cry out, the sensation almost too much to take.

Caleb growls as he bears down on my clit, sending waves of the hottest pleasure I've ever felt straight to my core.

"And I'm going to fuck you all night long," he

says as his tongue licks across my clit, "until you come for Daddy over and over again."

He slides his cock back into me, slowly rocking into me at first but then picking up speed.

He starts to fuck me in a furious rhythm, his thumb on my clit and his cock in my pussy, working together to drive me absolutely insane.

I can feel another orgasm building inside me like a hot, glowing furnace, and I know that it's going to be the best one yet.

I throw my head back and gasp as I feel Caleb's cock swell inside me.

He snarls like a beast as he starts to fuck me even harder.

"Come for Daddy," he growls. "Come for me, baby girl. Let Daddy feel you come."

"Caleb!" I shout as the orgasm tears through me, drowning out the rest of the world.

Caleb shudders and groans, his body tensing as he finds his own release inside me. "Motherfuck!"

His cock pulses and throbs as he roars out his climax, sending wave after wave of pleasure throughout my body until I'm sure I can't take anymore.

Finally, with one last shudder, Caleb collapses onto the bed beside me.

He wraps an arm around me, pulling me close until my head is resting on his chest.

I'm already falling into the most contented sleep of my life when I hear his whisper against my hair, "I'm never letting you go, angel."

Chapter Four

Caleb

I AWAKEN my sleeping beauty with my head between her legs. She moans and arches up into me as I lick and suck on her clit.

This is all the breakfast I'll ever need for the rest of my life.

"Caleb..." Heaven moans my name, and my cock jumps in response, moisture beading at the tip.

I slide my fingers into her pussy, feeling the wetness there.

My cock grows even harder. Fuck, she's so wet that I can slide two fingers in this time.

She moans and arches her back, pushing her

pussy against my hand, wanting more. I slide another finger in and pump them in and out of her.

"Fuck me, Daddy," she whispers.

With a growl, I slide my fingers out of her and lower my head to her pussy.

"I've found the promised land," I tell her as I stare at her little pink gash.

She whimpers, and I can see the moisture glistening on her sweet cunt, beckoning me. With a moan of pure pleasure, I lick her from clit to ass, then plunge my tongue inside her.

She bucks and moans as I eat her pussy, licking and sucking as I work my tongue in and out of her and massage her clit with my fingers.

"Yes, oh yes! Daddy!" she moans and whimpers like a little sex kitten, the sounds she's making driving me insane.

I slide my mouth down to her clit, sucking it into my mouth and rubbing it with my tongue as I slide my fingers in and out of her, moving faster and faster, in and out, in and out, and rubbing her clit, faster and faster, her moans and groans getting louder and louder.

I slide my tongue down her slit and find her ass, working my tongue in and out of her ass, too.

"Oh my god!" she screams just before I feel her pussy start to spasm around my fingers.

"Come for Daddy, baby girl," I whisper as I feel her juices gush all over my hand, her ass clenching and unclenching on my tongue.

"Caleb!" she screams my name as she comes, her pussy gushing all around my fingers, her ass squeezing my tongue.

Her pussy clenches and releases, clenches and releases.

She's trembling, moaning, and whimpering as she comes, her pussy still spasming around my fingers.

I continue to run my tongue in and out of her ass and finger fuck her pussy until she's spent.

When she finally stops shaking, I slowly and carefully withdraw my fingers from her pussy, licking her to get all her sweet juices. Then I slide up her body, kissing her stomach and her breasts and her neck, and then finally her mouth.

I take her mouth in a deep, passionate kiss, our tongues tangling together as we explore each other's mouths.

She tastes like sex and sweetness and Heaven, and I want to stay here in this moment forever.

I finally come up for air and lay my head on her

breasts, listening to the pounding of her heart, feeling the warmth of her skin under my hands.

My cock is still hard as a rock, demanding release, but I ignore it, preferring to revel in this moment and just hold her.

We both lay there silently for several minutes, just enjoying the feeling of being close to each other until Heaven finally breaks the silence.

"Daddy," she whispers, "I need you..."

I already know what she's asking for, but I want to hear her say it.

"You need what?" I ask her, my voice husky with lust.

She blushes. "I want you...to you know..."

I grin at her innocence. "You want me to what?" I whisper in her ear.

"To fuck me," she finally breathes.

Hot damn. Something about hearing this innocent girl talk dirty has my cock rocketing to new proportions.

"If my little girl wants this dick, then that's what she's going to get," I grunt as I claim her lips in another searing kiss.

"I want you on your hands and knees, baby," I whisper, my voice husky from lust.

She blushes but nods and rolls over so she's

on her hands and knees, her ass in the air, her pussy glistening in the low light from the window.

"Like that?" she glances back at me over her shoulders, her cheeks stained a pretty pink.

I groan. "Just like that, pretty girl."

I run my hand down her back until I reach the curve of her ass, and then I smack her hard.

I hear her gasp in surprise and then moan in pleasure, and I know she likes it.

I do it again and again, until her ass is red and hot, my cock leaking precum in anticipation.

I don't know what the hell's gotten into me. I've never been into this kind of shit, but it's her. She's pulling something deep and dark and forbidden out of me.

"Do you like that, baby?" I ask her in a hoarse voice as I smack her ass again.

"Yes, Daddy!" she moans. "I like it."

I groan at her eager response, my cock jumping as I smack her ass again and line my aching shaft up with her pussy. "Tell me what you want," I whisper in her ear.

She doesn't hold back this time. "I want you to fuck me. I want you to fuck me hard, Daddy," she moans.

"Beg me," I grunt, my cock throbbing at her words.

"Please, Daddy. Please fuck me. Please fuck your baby girl," she whispers.

One more sharp smack on her ass, and I roar as I push my cock into her pussy, not stopping until my balls slap against her.

She moans loudly, and I feel her pussy spasm around my cock, squeezing me like a vise, trying to milk me for all I'm worth.

I rock into her, again and again, her tight, hot pussy milking my cock, driving me fucking insane.

I cock a leg up over her back and fuck her even deeper, the angle changing and driving me even closer to the edge.

"Harder!" she moans, pushing back against me.

And I give it to her. I give her all I've got, pounding into her, over and over again.

She moans as I fuck her. "You like that, don't you?" I snarl at her. "You like your daddy to give it to you raw and dirty?"

She just whimpers in response.

I wrap my fingers around her throat and hold onto her while I wildly lick and kiss the nape of her neck. She's got me out of my mind. I'm huffing and puffing as I ride her like I'm going for broke.

I feel her pussy tightening around me before she screams, "I'm going to come!"

"Good girl," I grunt, slamming into her even harder. "Come all over your daddy's dick."

She cries out, and I feel her shudder and shake as she comes, her pussy gripping my cock like a vise, milking me for all I'm worth.

I slam into her once more and roar as I come hard and fast, pulse after pulse of hot, sticky cum shooting into her pussy, filling her up until it's running down her thighs.

I collapse against her and roll onto my back, pulling her with me.

She rolls over onto her side and snuggles up against me, her head on my chest.

We lay there in silence until I hear her breathing even out. It does funny things to my chest to know this innocent, perfect angel is sleeping trustingly in my arms.

I run my hand over her hair and kiss the top of her head.

Heaven might not fully realize it yet, but she's *mine*.

Only mine.

Chapter Five

Heaven

I NEVER THOUGHT I'd be having sex with a man I wasn't married to.

My father preaches against it.

The people in my father's church would be scandalized.

I'm scandalized.

I do it anyway.

I know that according to what my father preaches about, what I'm doing with Caleb is wrong. We're having sex out of wedlock.

No, we're not just having sex.

We're *fucking*.

It's raw and hot and dirty and twisted and forbidden.

I call him *daddy,* and he calls me his *little girl.*

And God help me, but just thinking about it gets me all hot and bothered and throbbing.

I don't care if it's wrong. It feels so *right.*

When I went home, I lied to my father and told him I was staying at a friend's house. He shook his head at me disapprovingly and berated me for not telling him where I was and making him worry. If he could have grounded me, I know he would have, but I'm eighteen, so he can't.

I don't know why I keep staying here with him. I could just leave. I could just stay with Caleb all the time. I know he wants me to.

But my heart skips a beat when I think of how he's on the run, living hidden away for a crime he didn't commit.

He hasn't told me all the details, and I don't need to know them. I know Caleb. I trust him implicitly. He's innocent. I know it as surely as I know the sky is blue.

And if I just disappear and start staying with him, I take the risk of leading the authorities to him. I can't do that to him.

So, I sneak out every chance I get and meet him

in the woods where he leads me the rest of the way to his cabin.

Our getaway. Our little hole in the universe where we can pretend I'm not a preacher's daughter, and he's not a wanted man.

A world where he's my daddy and I'm his little girl...

I shiver as I think that, and Caleb tightens his hold on me, kissing my shoulder.

I feel his cock twitch inside me, still hard, and I know I'm not done yet.

He thrusts hard and fast, and I clench hard around him, riding my orgasm out. "Daddy!" I cry out and then bite my hand to keep quiet. I don't want anyone to hear us. I don't want to get caught.

Even though I know no one can hear us out here in the middle of nowhere in Caleb's cabin.

I can't help but feel like we're doing something illicit. Wrong. Even though what we do is consensual and we're in love.

But even thinking about the word "love" makes me feel guilty. Guilt is supposed to be reserved for when you do something wrong. You don't feel guilt for anything you do that's right. And I'm not wrong for Caleb. He's not wrong for me.

And I know my father only wants what's best for me, and he's only trying to protect me.

I trust Caleb, and I love him. That has to count for something.

"Oh, fuck, honey," Caleb groans from the small taste of heaven that I give him, and he comes hard inside me. I feel his cock twitch and throb, filling me up with his cum.

I blissfully bask in the afterglow as Caleb slowly eases his cock out of me. I can feel his cum dribbling out of me, down the crack of my ass, and I grind my hips against him to spread it around.

I lay back against the pillows, my mind reeling.

What the fuck are we going to do?

I feel Caleb kiss my shoulder and then lay down next to me. He pulls me against him and kisses my forehead.

I love him so much. How can I deny my feelings now?

But I know my father won't allow this once he finds out.

Caleb strokes the side of my face, ever intuitive. He already knows I'm bothered before I say anything.

"What are you thinking about?" he asks, his voice guarded.

"That it's not fair," I answer honestly. "My father isn't going to let this continue when he finds out, Caleb."

Caleb's arms tighten around me possessively as he growls, "Don't you worry about that, baby. No one is going to take you away from me."

I shake my head and push away from Caleb gently. "But, Caleb, you're wanted for murder. If anyone finds out about us, then you're exposed. Me being here with you is dangerous to you."

Caleb reaches for me again, but I quickly scoot away from him and jump up out of the bed before he can grab me and make me change my mind with his body.

"Heaven," he says my voice like a warning, but I'm already shutting down, the tears forming in my eyes as I hastily get dressed.

I know what I have to do, and it's going to be hard enough without hearing Caleb beg me not to.

I feel Caleb come up behind me, but I bolt just out of his reach before he can wrap his arms around me. If he does that, I'll melt back into him and cave, and I can't do that.

If I really love him, I have to put his safety first, and I take the risk of leading the authorities to him every time I visit him like this.

"Please, Caleb, I have to go," I tell him without meeting his eyes.

"You're coming back?" he asks me, a hint of desperation in his voice.

"Yes," I lie, still without meeting his eyes, "but I have to go now. I'm going to be late to church, and then my father will come looking for me."

"Heaven..."

Caleb calls my name again, but I'm already sprinting out the door like the devil himself is on my heels.

I'm not strong enough to withstand the temptation that is Caleb. Part of it is that I don't want to.

No matter how much I might need to.

For both his sake and mine.

Chapter Six

Caleb

SHE LIED TO ME.

She couldn't meet my eyes because she was afraid I'd see it, but, hell, she didn't even have to look at me.

I could hear it in her voice.

Heaven doesn't understand that I've studied everything about her. I know every hitch in her voice, every slight movement of her body.

She can never hide from me.

Every day when she sneaks back to her father's house, she doesn't know that I'm there with her.

I follow her everywhere she goes now. It's stupid

as fuck. Every moment that I spend in that little town in Tennessee puts me closer behind bars, but how can I stay hidden out in my cabin in the mountains when my angel is out there all alone? Unprotected. Without her daddy to take care of her.

She *needs* me.

I need *her*.

No way I'm leaving her alone. No sir.

So, I follow her now, intent on making sure she makes it back to her father's house okay. Then, I'll sit outside and stare at her window all night. I'll follow her to church and peep through the church house window at her like I've been doing ever since the day I met and claimed her as mine.

She's mine, dammit. *Mine*!

If it wasn't for this bogus charge, I could strut right inside that church and let the whole damn town know it.

Fuck them and their holier-than-thou attitudes. I'd bend Heaven right over that altar and fuck her to kingdom come in front of all of them just to show everyone who her daddy is and to let all those dirty motherfuckers know just what they're missing.

What they can never have.

I'm a deranged fucker.

But, fuck, Heaven makes me that way.

I stare at the door as she steps out with her father. My mouth goes dry at the sight of her.

She's wearing a long-sleeved white dress that falls down to just above her knees, looking sweeter and more innocent than the virgin Mary herself.

The thoughts I'm having about her right now are damn near blasphemous, but I can't help it.

I go insane just at the sight of her.

I follow her and her father to the little church he pastors, and then I take up my perch outside one of the church windows. No one can see me peeping in, but I've got a perfect view of Heaven's pretty face.

Her perfect body.

Those long, bare legs.

I bite back a growl when I see all the old men in the church peeking glances at her.

Dirty fucking perverts. Sanctimonious assholes, the lot of them. I see the lust in their eyes.

My nostrils flare. I know what they're thinking. They're all imagining what it would be like to stuff their cocks inside her, and that knowledge is nearly enough to make me barge in there right now—consequences be damned.

Heaven sits with the choir, her pretty pink lips moving in song, and my cock hardens in my pants when I remember the way they were wrapped around my cock just earlier today.

Precum starts leaking from my tip, and I palm myself through my jeans, trying to stop the sudden aching in my balls as I continue to stare at my girl.

It doesn't go away, though. My balls just get heavier and heavier. I don't know how the fuck I'm able to produce so much sperm, but Heaven has my body on overload. My balls are boiling with cum, ready to go every time I see her.

Heaven's little tongue snakes out to glide over her bottom lip, and my cock jerks painfully.

Fuck it.

I unzip my pants and take my aching length in my hand.

Yeah, I know I'm standing outside the church, jacking off as I peep in at the preacher's daughter. This isn't the first time I've done it, and I'm sure it won't be the last. I felt guilty the first time I did it, but I stopped caring the second time I shot my load all over the side of the building.

I figure I'm busting hell wide open now anyway. Might as well enjoy the trip there.

Heaven's little pink tongue darts out again, and I groan as I stroke myself.

I picture my cum splashing against that pretty face of hers.

I almost come when I picture her licking it from her lips.

She looks over to me, her eyes lighting with surprise when they meet mine through the window.

The rest of the world fades away as her eyes stare into mine.

I can see the lust in those deep, brown eyes. She wants me.

She wants my seed on her face.

She wants me to breed her.

She's my mate, and I'm going to claim her.

I'm going to fuck her until she can't walk, and then I'm going to fuck her some more.

I'm going to run my hands down that body of hers —showing it off to everyone at the fucking church.

One of these days...

One of these days...everyone's going to know she's mine.

And then, I'm going to breed her.

I come all over the side of the church, every muscle in my neck taut as I throw my head back and bite my tongue to contain my roar of release.

My chest is heaving as I struggle to stand. I bring

my hand up to wipe my seed off the stone of the church.

I've never been so turned on in my life.

My eyes meet Heaven's again through the church window.

Her cheeks are flushed. Her little chest is heaving up and down.

My gaze flicks to the men in the congregation. Red, hot anger wells up inside me when I see many of them adjusting their bulging erections.

They're like a pack of hungry wolves. They can sense the change in her. They can smell her desire. Their lecherous eyes are roving over my girl's ripe, young body, undressing her in their minds.

I finally do let out my roar then.

Hell fucking no.

I don't think. I just react, following my instincts.

I kick in the door of the church and start barging up the aisle.

I'm going to claim my woman come hell or high water.

Satan himself couldn't stop me.

Chapter Seven

Caleb

HEAVEN GASPS when she sees me storming up the aisle. She's never seen me like this before. My jaw is clenched tight, and I'm sure my eyes are ablaze with raw determination.

The other congregation members look on in shock as I march past them, my strides purposeful and unwavering.

I take Heaven's arm and tug her toward me. I can see the confusion in her eyes, her lips parting as though she wants to say something, but I don't give her the chance.

I grab her hand and pull her out of the church, ignoring the murmurs of the congregation.

I don't know where the fuck her father is, and I can't truly say I care. He'd better keep his ass away if he doesn't want to see something he shouldn't.

The freshness of the night air hits us as we step outside. I'm nearly sprinting as I lead her away from the church to a secluded spot behind some trees.

Once there, she looks up at me, her eyes wide with fear and anticipation. I know she's not afraid of me. My darling girl is afraid *for* me. She worries about me. She cares about me in a way no one else ever has.

No one else has ever given a damn what happens to me.

But this angel does.

She knows what I'm going to do. Her lips part in a contented sigh as I take her face in my hands and look into her eyes before I take her lips in a passionate kiss.

Her lips tremble against mine, and I can feel the heat radiating from her body.

No one else exists in this moment. It's just the two of us.

I bring my hand up and tangle my fingers in her hair, deepening the kiss, wanting to consume her.

I can feel her body trembling as my hands start to roam, exploring her curves and touching her in ways she's never been touched before.

I can feel the fire burning between us and I know that she can feel it too.

"Unhand her right now, son!" her father's voice booms from behind me.

I turn to face the preacher, standing protectively in front of Heaven.

"Like hell I will," I tell him and the group of church members that followed him out. They're all standing in front of me with frowns like an angry mob out to save the damsel in distress from an ogre. Only thing they lack is the pitchforks.

And the fact that this damsel doesn't want to be rescued. No, she wants me all up in that cunt. Guarantee she's soaking fucking wet for it right now too.

The pastor holds his cell phone up. "You might as well go ahead and give it up, son. The authorities are on their way. We all know who you are. Now, unhand my daughter."

"No," Heaven suddenly pipes up from behind me.

The preacher's brow furrows as Heaven steps out from behind me and clasps her tiny hand in mine. "No?" he questions her with a raised eyebrow, his eyes flicking down to where she's joined our hands.

"I love him, Dad," Heaven pronounces, her chin lifted as she holds her father's gaze defiantly.

My brave, beautiful girl. My chest swells with emotion at the way she's standing up for me in front of the whole town.

Her father frowns, his lips thinning. "I forbid it," he snaps before he points his finger at the ground. "Get over here, young lady," he orders like she's a dog.

My nostrils flare as a surge of protectiveness rises up within me. I can't stop the growl from rumbling up out of my throat, but Heaven places a reassuring hand on my chest as she straightens her spine and says firmly, "No."

I hear the collective gasp from the crowd. Jesus, has no one in this town ever told the preacher no before? Hell, they act like he's God himself or something.

"I'll be damned if my daughter is going to be with a murderer."

More gasps from the crowd. Guess they've never heard the preacher curse before.

"Careful, preacher," I caution him. "You're slipping."

The man's face gets as red as a tomato when he realizes his blunder.

"Ah, about time," he says as the authorities come pushing their way through the crowd, intent on getting to me.

The preacher turns to them and orders, "Arrest this man!"

I can feel Heaven's body shaking beside me as the officers cuff me, but I keep my gaze forward and my jaw clenched tight. It was worth it. A few moments of passion between us was better than a lifetime of living with regrets.

"Wait!"

My head snaps up, a denial already on my lips as I see my sister pushing through the crowd.

"Ariana..." I warn.

Tears shine in my sister's eyes as she suddenly blurts, "It wasn't my brother! It was me! I did it."

I shut my eyes in resignation as the wood becomes so quiet all that can be heard is the rustling of a squirrel in a nearby tree.

"I killed Martin Finley," she cries, her voice breaking. "He raped me. It was self-defense, but Caleb took the fall because he didn't want to put me through the shame of having to relive it."

Her voice drops to barely more than a whisper.

"I'm so sorry. I didn't want to have to tell everyone. I didn't want to have to talk about it on a witness stand."

Ariana looks at me now, her blonde hair pressed against her tear-stained face. "I'm so sorry, Caleb. I shouldn't have let you take the fall for me. I should have been braver."

I don't say anything. I just shake my head at her.

The chief of police steps forward, eyeing me harshly. "Is this true?"

The cat's out of the bag now, so I look him square in the eye as I give one curt nod.

He stares at me for a long moment, no doubt trying to assess whether I'm telling the truth or not.

He must decide that I am because a moment later, he orders my release with a wave of his hand at his officers.

The cuffs slide off my wrist, and Heaven immediately leaps into my arms.

I hold her close to me and kiss the top of her head.

"Wait!" The preacher sputters. "Are you just going to let him go?"

The chief of police turns to him. "Got no reason to hold him now, Sir." He nods to my sister. "This young lady has confessed."

Ariana is still crying as she finally tells the truth about what happened. A couple of female officers are taking her statement, all while reassuring her that everything's going to be okay.

My shoulders relax. So long as my sister isn't going to be arrested and is going to be okay, I can rest easy with her decision to divulge the truth.

"Heaven, you will honor my wishes," the preacher turns his angry eyes back to his daughter.

"No, I won't." Her voice doesn't even waver this time. "Caleb is innocent. There's no reason for you to forbid me from being with him."

"I am your father!" he hisses.

"Yes, but Caleb is my daddy," she practically purrs as she turns those innocent eyes up to me.

And just like that, my cock is at full mast again. The fact that Heaven is calling me daddy in front of her father and the entire congregation does something to me.

Her legs wrap around my waist as I hoist her up into my arms right here in front of everyone. I don't give a fuck who's watching. I need her *now*.

"Oh, fuck, sweet baby. Daddy needs you," I breathe into her ear as she begins humping me through our clothing, sliding that sweet little mound up and down my throbbing length in front of everyone.

Heaven's actions are driving me wild with desire. I need to feel her naked skin against mine, to taste her sweet mouth, to make love to her right here in front of everyone.

She knows exactly what I'm thinking, and she whimpers, a sound of pure need.

It sets my blood to boiling.

She's not only my lover and my submissive, but she's also my soulmate. We have a deep connection that goes beyond physical pleasure.

As much as I want to fuck her right here and now, I'm a jealous bastard. I can't stand the thought of any of these men seeing her beautiful body—even if it is while I'm laying claim to it.

They don't deserve to see her purity. Hell, I don't deserve it, but I count myself the luckiest man alive that I have it, and there's no way in hell I'm going to share it.

So, I carry her to my car. She's still moaning and whining and humping me desperately, causing precum to froth up out of my tip.

When we finally reach my car, I lay her down on the back seat. I climb on top of her, and we continue where we left off.

We kiss passionately, our tongues exploring each other's mouths. I can feel her body writhing beneath me as I tease her nipples with my fingertips.

"Caleb," she moans my name, and I groan in response.

"Sshh, Daddy knows, baby. I know what you need, and I'm going to give it to you, honey. Don't you worry."

I'm hard and ready for her, and she knows it. She reaches down and unzips my pants, freeing my aching cock. I groan when it bobs free.

She strokes it gently at first, then with increasing pressure.

I groan as she takes me in her mouth, her lips sliding up and down my shaft. She's already an expert at this, and I can feel myself getting closer to the edge, but I don't want to come yet. I want to be inside her.

I pull her up and kiss her deeply as I slide into her wet, warm depths. She's so tight around me, and I can feel her muscles contracting as I thrust into her.

We're both moaning and panting, lost in the pleasure. I can't believe we're doing this in broad daylight in a public place. But it only turns me on more.

I don't care where we are. "I need you to distraction. You know that?" I rasp in her ear. "You drive me fucking insane, Heaven Leigh."

I grab her hips and force her harder against me. She's making whimpering noises. I feel her walls clenching around me, and I know she's close.

"Caleb, I'm so close," she pants.

"Come for me, baby. Come on my cock."

She moans again, this time her whole body shivering while she comes. I feel her walls clenching around me and I let go, coming harder than I ever have in my entire life.

When we're done, she collapses against the seat, breathing heavily.

I keep my cock lodged inside her as I gather her onto my lap.

I stroke her hair and all along her back, marveling at this perfect beauty that's mine.

Mine.

All mine.

Epilogue

Five Years Later

Heaven

I PUT the kids to bed and quietly tiptoe down the hallway to the bedroom where my husband awaits me.

Caleb is everything I never even knew I wanted or needed. We have two beautiful children—a boy and a girl, and life couldn't be better.

We decided to expand on Caleb's cabin here in the woods. We're not too far from the town for when we need supplies, and Caleb is a competent huntsman and fisherman, so he catches a lot of our meals himself. He also sells meat to the local markets.

For my part, I make jams and jellies from the berries I gather and sell them to the local stores.

We're not rich by any means, but we have more than enough to get by, and most importantly, we're happy.

I don't talk to my father anymore. He couldn't ever get over me dishonoring him, but I don't care. If the way to honor him was to give up Caleb, I'm glad I dishonored him.

Caleb and our family are my everything, and I wouldn't trade them for the world.

When I reach our bedroom, my husband meets me at the door.

My heart melts at the love in his eyes, while my breath catches at the desire I see in them.

He wordlessly takes my hand and leads me over to the window overlooking the mountains. He's got all the lights off. The only light illuminating the space is that of the moon glinting off the mountains and shining in through the window.

He drops to his knees before me and pushes my dress up.

"Been waiting all day to lick my baby's pretty pussy," Caleb breathes, his breath fanning across my sensitive mound before he rakes his warm tongue across my clit.

I moan, my head falling back as my fingers fist in his hair.

My husband knows I like to be eaten out before we have sex, and he loves to eat my pussy as much as I love for him to do it.

It's a win-win.

"You wanna ride me, baby?" Caleb asks between kisses to my trembling stomach, his hands sliding up the backs of my thighs to hook under my ass.

"Yes," I moan, sliding my hands down the soft hair of his beard.

He stands and turns me, so I'm facing the window.

Then he bends me over the sill of the window, my ass sticking out and my head down, looking at the moonlit mountains.

His big, straining cock finds my entrance and slides in.

"Yes," I breathe, my hips already moving to receive him. "Yes, please, Daddy!" I'm trying to be quiet so we don't wake the kids. I bite my hand to silence the loud moan that threatens to tear up out of me when I feel Caleb bottom out inside me.

"Oh, fuck," he whispers. I can tell he's trying to be quiet too.

Caleb is slow at first, but his pace quickly picks up as he thrusts into me from behind. His hands dig into my hips, and he groans above me.

He pounds into me.

I wish I could look at my husband, and I wish I could look out the window, but I leave my eyes closed, my head bowed as I take in every sensation.

The moon, the stars, the early evening breeze all wash over me, adding to the pleasure my husband is gifting me with.

He thrusts harder and faster, and all I know is the man I adore and the pleasure he brings me.

"Caleb, I'm going to come," I pant, ramming my hips back against him.

He spanks my ass. One sharp slam. "Nu-uh. You know what to call me when I'm balls deep inside this hot pussy."

Oh my god. My pussy instantly clenches in response as I confess, "Daddy!"

I'm whisper-yelling, trying to be quiet, but the pleasure is climbing higher and higher.

Caleb senses it and silences me by wrapping a hand over my mouth.

His head falls into the crook of my neck. He

groans directly into my ear as I feel his hot fluid spraying into me.

It's a groan of pure, masculine pleasure, and it's enough to set off my own orgasm.

I scream against his hand as my pussy falls apart on him.

"Yes, that's it, baby," Caleb rasps in my ear as he continues to ride me through our orgasms. "Come all over your daddy's cock, baby. Give it to me."

Caleb keeps moving in me, pulling two, three, four orgasms from me until I collapse in his arms.

He catches me before I hit the floor and carries me over to the bed where he gathers me close to his chest and holds me while he whispers words of love and possession in my ears.

"My Heaven," are the last words I hear him whisper before I drift off to sleep in his arms, safe and warm.

And I am his.

Always and forever.

Want more Emma Bray? Get a free book at www.authoremmabray.com.

www.ingramcontent.com/pod-product-compliance
Lightning Source LLC
Chambersburg PA
CBHW021352160726
47994CB00007B/2935